# THE
# JOURNEY
# WITH
# JONAH

# THE
# JOURNEY
# WITH
# JONAH

## Madeleine L'Engle

WITH ILLUSTRATIONS BY
LEONARD EVERETT FISHER

A Sunburst Book

Farrar, Straus and Giroux

Text copyright © 1967 by Madeleine L'Engle Franklin
Illustrations copyright © 1967 by Leonard Everett Fisher
All rights reserved
Library of Congress catalog card number: 67-19885
Published in Canada by HarperCollins*CanadaLtd*
Printed in the United States of America
First edition, 1967
Noonday Press edition, 1978
Sunburst edition, 1991

For Theron

THE
JOURNEY
WITH
JONAH

Once upon a time when the earth was younger and time was slower and it took three days to cross from one end to the other of Nineveh, that great city, there lived in the village of Gath-hepher a prophet named Jonah.

Now Jonah was, like many prophets, an angry man.

Well: just look at him! There he sits, cross-legged, his prophet's robes bunched up about him. He is perched atop a small rock on the crest of a hill overlooking Gath-hepher, and he is angry, as usual, and talking very loudly to someone.

To whom is he talking? Not to the animals who are surrounding him at a respectful distance, nor to the birds standing interestedly under the nearest tree. No: he is talking up at a small white cloud in a very large blue sky, but he is not talking to the cloud.

Listen:

And I do well to be angry, Lord,
I do very well.
It is a most unreasonable demand you have made.
Why did you come to me and say
"Arise, go to Nineveh, that great city,
And cry against it,
For their wickedness is come upon me"?
Why should I arise, O Lord?
Why don't you appoint a prophet from Nineveh?
All right, don't tell me. I know why.
You don't have a prophet there.
You aren't their god, that's why.
So why should I arise and go to Nineveh?

[*He raises one arm in its flowing, prophet's sleeve, and points towards the village*]

Here I am, looking down on Gath-hepher,
Gath-hepher, my own village.
What's wrong with Gath-hepher?
Or, rather, what's right with it?
There's a great deal wrong with Gath-hepher, Lord.
I don't need to tell you the things that are wrong with
    it (do I?).
All the usual things.
You know them perfectly well.
People gamble and steal and cheat.
They go roaring about with too much wine in their
    bellies
And they beat their wives
And their children play hooky from school.

And that's only the least of it.
I leave the rest to your imagination, Lord,
And you have plenty of that.
It took imagination to dream up sending me to warn
The people of Nineveh.
Why Nineveh, Nineveh of all places?
Why can't I warn the people of Gath-hepher?
They're my own people.
Not only that, they're your people.
You chose us.
Aren't you forgetting that?
It seems to me that's a most important point to re-
    member.
Lord?
*I won't go to Nineveh!*


GOOSE

[*To* OWL]

Did he?


OWL

[*Looking at* GOOSE *in annoyance through his wise, spectacled eyes*]

Did who what?


GOOSE

Did God choose them?


OWL

Indubitably.

### JAY

[*Responding to the* GOOSE'S *sigh*]

All he means is: yes, without doubt. Go on, Jonah! You tell him.

### JONAH

[*Looks around, but* JAY *pretends she hasn't said a word.* JONAH *returns to his tirade to the sky*]

It's too far away in the first place.
In the second place I hate cities.
And in the third place,
Now pay attention to this, Lord, this is important,
In the third place Nineveh is the enemy.
You know that perfectly well. They hate us.
They don't want a Hebrew prophet coming to warn them
About anything.
They won't like it.
*And neither do I.*
You're not even their god. You're ours.
I quite understand that people need to be warned.
So I'll do that much for you.
I'll warn the people of Gath-hepher.

### JAY

[*She has been listening with great interest, and now she hops closer to* JONAH. *She is a very pretty bird, and sure of her own charms*]

Uh—by the way, Jonah, who are you talking to?

[*But* JONAH *is paying no attention to the Bluejay. He is practicing warning*]

JONAH

You are a bad, a terrible, a faithless girl. Your wickedness is come up before me.

JAY

[*Indignantly*]

What's this rubbish? I'm an excellent, a diligent, a dutiful girl, and I asked who you were talking to.

JONAH

[*Finally focusing on her*]

I wasn't talking to anybody. I was practicing. In any case, the point is not to whom I was talking, but who was talking to me.

JAY

You were making so much noise that whoever it was couldn't get in a word edgewise.

JONAH

Don't be impudent.

OWL

In any event, O prodigious prophet,

[JONAH *likes the adjective*]

do you think he will be satisfied with another local prophecy?

[ 8 ]

JONAH

Why shouldn't he be? He asked me to prophesy, so I'm
going to prophesy. Right here in Gath-hepher. And what
business is it of yours? Must I be a brother to dragons and
a companion to owls?

JAY

Now don't be so cranky, prophet. There isn't a dragon
among us and if you'll stop scowling at us I'll tell you why
I came to see you.

JONAH

*You* came to see *me?*

JAY

Actually I brought a few of my friends.

JONAH

Am I peculiar? Everybody wants a good laugh, is that it?

JAY

[*Slyly placating*]

They've never seen anybody famous before.

JONAH

[*Beginning to pay more attention*]

Famous?

[*Then he catches himself up*]

Flattery is the fall of prophets.

It isn't every village has a prophet. It isn't even every century has a prophet.

[*To the other birds*]

All right, you can look. But don't touch.

[*She sounds like a teacher taking a group of schoolchildren through a museum.* OWL *is offended, but* CATBIRD *and* GOOSE *come closer*]

Jonah: Owl. Owl: Jonah. Jonah, as you all know, did the prophesying for King Jeroboam the Second.

OWL

Israel first, eh, Jonah?

JONAH

What?

OWL

It is not inappropriate for the personal prophet of King Jeroboam to have a tendency to safeguard national interests.

JAY

[*Explaining for the bewildered* GOOSE]

Charity begins at home.

[*As this doesn't help, she continues*]

King Jeroboam the Second is king around here, and Jonah went and prophesied for him. But there's still lots to do right here at home, so why should he go prophesy for Nineveh before we've taken care of ourselves? I think you're quite right, O Jonah, son of Amittai. If you go and cry against Nineveh, that great city, what will happen to us?

#### OWL

It is not essential that we have emotions of personal approbation for individuals in order to apprehend them of the unmitigated wrathfulness of the Lord's intentions.

#### GOOSE

[*Wistfully*]

I wish I knew what he was talking about.

#### CATBIRD

[*Languidly*]

He is saying you don't have to like people to warn them.

#### GOOSE

Oh. Oh, I see. Thank you.

#### CATBIRD

Not at all.

#### JAY

Jonah: Goose. Goose: Jonah. Jonah: Catbird. Cat: Jonah.

[*They bow*]

#### GOOSE

Is he a real prophet?

Yes, and a profitable one.

[*Pointedly ignoring* CATBIRD]

The national program of territorial enlargement carried out by Jeroboam the Second was instigated by the prophet.

[*Explaining for the thoroughly bewildered* GOOSE]

Jonah's first successful prophecy, goosey, was to go to King Jeroboam and tell him to go into battle with the Assyrians and reclaim some of the land they'd taken from us in the first place. Which he did. Is that quite clear?

B-but what do the Assyrians have to do with Nineveh, Jay?

Nineveh is the capital of Assyria, Goose, and I don't blame Jonah one bit for not wanting to warn them. They're nasty, wicked people.

The Assyrian came down like a wolf on the fold.

[*Not catching the allusion*]

And the people of Gath-hepher are better?

JAY

No, they're nasty, wicked people too. But they're us. That makes all the difference.

GOOSE

Well, of course, I do believe in being patriotic. I mean, if there's going to be any warning done, it does seem right that it should be done to our own selves and not to strangers.

JAY

So you will warn the people of Gath-hepher, won't you, Jonah?

JONAH

I said I would.

CATBIRD

It's not so much that he isn't willing to be his brother's keeper, as that he quite naturally feels he has a right to choose just who his brother is.

JONAH

[Pleased; expansively]

After I warn Gath-hepher I might even go over to Nazareth. They don't have a prophet there.

GOOSE

That's a good idea. There'll never be a prophet come out of Nazareth.

JAY

How are you going to warn them in Gath-hepher?

CATBIRD

Or Nineveh, if you went there, which we know you won't?

GOOSE

Or Nazareth, poor things.

JONAH

[*Cross again. He doesn't like being pushed*]

I don't know. Go away. Leave me alone. I have indignation. I mean indigestion. Everybody is wicked in Gath-hepher. Even the cattle and the kine and the beasts of the field and

[*He whirls on them*]

the fowls of the air.

CATBIRD

Are you warning us, perchance?

JONAH

If you want to take it that way.

GOOSE

[*Nervously*]

Us?

OWL

Silence, Goose. He knows that it would be redundant to warn us. We are what we are by nature, not by folly, nor by fall. It was only man who was driven out of Paradise.


GOOSE

I wish he'd talk so I knew what he was saying.


JONAH

I wish he wouldn't talk at all. It's a waste of my time sitting around chattering with birds.

[*He rises and takes what he considers a proper prophet's pose*]

Fowl! I *am* warning you! When you settled in villages and cast in your lot with men, you lost your place in Paradise and your right not to be warned. So heed me. I am going in to Gath-hepher. They regard lying vanities.

[*He strides off in the direction of the village. The birds don't quite dare follow him, but they flutter and fly up to the rock, where they can observe him better*]

O wicked generation in Gath-hepher, many sorrows shall be to your wickedness. You are like the beasts that perish. You give your mouths to evil, your tongues frame deceit—

[*His words fade off as he plunges downhill*]


JAY

Not bad! He's not bad at all.


OWL

Even if totally unoriginal.

CATBIRD

He does have a flair, a style, that I can't help admiring.

JAY

In any case, prophets aren't supposed to be original. A warning is a warning.

GOOSE

Oh—oh—Jay—look—

CATBIRD

The children are chasing him down the street!
The dogs are nipping at his feet!
The prophet in Gath-hepher is scorned.

GOOSE

The people don't seem to want to be warned.

OWL

A certain amount of responsible action on our part to prevent further reprehensible atrocities to our prophet seems to be indicated.

GOOSE

But we're only birds. We'd be caught and eaten.

CATBIRD

Look at the prophet! He's being beaten!

GOOSE

They're throwing eggs!

[ 17 ]

CATBIRD

They're throwing stones!

GOOSE

If they don't watch out, they'll break his bones!

JAY

I feel personally responsible. I'm going after him. If I
don't come back I want a proper funeral with a full choir.

[*She flitters off*]

OWL

Her impulsiveness is always getting that intemperate Jay
into difficulties and dilemmas. Moderation is an acquisi-
tion of character urgently to be desired.

GOOSE

Where's she gone? What's she doing? Oh, he's coming
back. Oh, oh, I can hardly bear to look.

[JONAH *comes up the hill. He is dirty. His clothes are torn.
The* OWL, GOOSE, *and* CATBIRD *keep a discreet distance. He
ignores them, speaking heavenwards*]

JONAH

Now don't tell me you're angry with *me*, Lord.
I thought it was worth trying, that's all.
You wanted me to warn, and I warned.
I thought it would please you if they repented of
their wickedness.

And I have no intention of going to Nineveh.
Sometimes you ask too much.
Even you have to have a sense of moderation, Lord.
You ought not to make unreasonable demands.
You must not expect trees to bear fruit out of season.

[*The* GOOSE *comes a little closer.* JONAH *ignores it pointedly*]

And wasn't it you, Lord, who said
Touch not mine anointed
And do my prophets no harm?


#### GOOSE

We're sorry, prophet. We didn't know they'd throw things at you.


#### OWL

The uncouthness of the residents of Gath-hepher is one of the considerations that kept me from settling here sooner.


#### JAY

[*Coming back up the hill, preening herself and looking quite self-satisfied*]

Fruit and vegetables I understand. Or even a rotten egg, as long as it's not one of mine. But throwing a stone is something else.


#### CATBIRD

A prophet is not without honor, save in his own country.

OWL

[*Examining* JONAH]

A slight abrasion, plus a minor contusion—

JONAH

Oh, be quiet. My head aches.

JAY

[*Sidling up to him*]

I brought you something.

[*Coaxing*]

It's a present. It'll make you feel better.

JONAH

[*Not turning; not looking*]

What is it?

JAY

Under my left wing or my right?

JONAH

No games.

GOOSE

Oh, go on! Guess!

JAY

It's nice.

[*And, as she still gets no response*]

It's an earring. For you.

[*Turns around. Reaches for it. Stops*]
Where did you get it?

JAY
[*Evading*]
I got it for you.

JONAH
Take it back.

JAY
But he was the one who threw the stone.

JONAH
Take it back.

JAY
He probably stole it.

JONAH
And you?

JAY
I *took* it. That's quite different. It's in my nature. And the
whole point of taking it was to give it, not take it.

[ 21 ]

CATBIRD

She can talk herself out of almost anything.


JONAH

I cannot stand stealing.


JAY

That's a big word for a very small earring.


JONAH

O bird, it is a foul thing that you have done.


CATBIRD

After all, she is a fowl.


JONAH

*Be quiet!*

All right, Lord. I get the point. You don't want me to warn the people of Gath-hepher. You don't want me to stay in Gath-hepher. So you've sent these foolish birds to drive me away. All right. I'm going.


JAY

But where are you going, Jonah, son of Amittai?


JONAH

Away.


GOOSE

But where?

OWL

Nineveh, perchance?

JONAH

I am not going to Nineveh. Let us all get that straight.

JAY

But where, then, Jonah?

JONAH

To the farthest corners of the earth. Away from Gath-hepher. Away from voices in my ear, yours, or—or any-body's.

JAY

You won't take the earring? For luck?

JONAH

No, fowl. I am going away from your presents and your presence. And His.

[*He strides off, casting one glance back at the sky. The* JAY *pauses to put on the earring, saying, "Come on," to the other birds as the Rat family comes on from the opposite direction. They are* MOTHER RAT, FATHER RAT, *and the three little rats,* HUZ, BUZ, *and* HAZO. *The parents are having a heated discus-sion*]

MOTHER RAT

Please be quiet, papa. A public dock in Joppa is no place for you to raise your voice.

#### FATHER RAT

[*Bellowing*]

I am being quiet!

#### MOTHER RAT

I have no intention of packing up. We're nicely settled in and I see no reason to leave. This is by far the most comfortable ship we've sailed with for a long time.

#### FATHER RAT

I'm warning you, mama, I've traveled in ships for longer than you have, and I know when it's time to leave.

#### MOTHER RAT

I'm tired of your thinking you know everything and never letting me have my own way. We've stayed in Joppa long enough—

#### FATHER RAT

There are other ships.

#### MOTHER RAT

But not going to Tarshish. The children have never been to Tarshish. You want to go to Tarshish, don't you, children?

#### LITTLE RATS

Yes, mama.

#### FATHER RAT

I'm only thinking of their safety.

But we're hungry, papa.

And you saw all the food the sailors stowed in the hold this morning.

We need our vitamins. Mama says so.

They're growing children and they must have balanced meals.

And I'm warning you, mama, that if we go on this ship we won't have any kind of meals for long. Just drink. Much too much to drink.

That's not funny, papa. I tell you this ship is in excellent condition. The seams have been freshly caulked, the wood is sound, and the weather forecast is excellent.

And I tell you, mama, that this ship smells like a sinking ship and it's time to leave. Don't trust your stomach, woman, trust your nose.

I don't believe in running away from things. What's to be

will be, and running away isn't going to change it. You could be eaten by a cat right here on dry land in Joppa.

FATHER RAT

All right, woman, have it your own way. But you'll regret it.

MOTHER RAT

Come on, children, everything's settled. Papa says we can go.

[JONAH *comes on and crosses the stage*]

HUZ

A funny man just came on the ship, mama.

BUZ

He went up the gangplank.

HAZO

He looked mad.

MOTHER RAT

Come along, children. Stop gossiping with the paying passengers. The sailors are pulling up the anchor. Hurry up now before we get left behind.

[*The rats scurry about, settling in. Almost immediately there comes a flash of lightning and a crash of thunder*]

FATHER RAT

I told you so.

HUZ

I feel funny.


BUZ

I'm seasick.


MOTHER RAT

It's just a squall. It won't last long.


FATHER RAT

Long enough to send us to a watery grave.


HAZO

I'm scared.


FATHER RAT

Mark my words, there's a Jonah on board.


MOTHER RAT

Papa, that's an anachronism. Anyhow, you're frightening
the children. Be quiet.


FATHER RAT

This is no thunder shower, mama.


MOTHER RAT

Stop squalling, papa.


FATHER RAT

The sailors are all praying to their gods.


[ 28 ]

MOTHER RAT

Then there'll be no harm in our praying to our god, too.
Come on, children, touch your claws, turn up your whiskers, and say your prayers.

[*They squeak together*]

Great Rodent
Take thy trident
Calm the seas
And afterwards please
Give us our cheese.

HUZ

It's getting worse.

BUZ

I don't like it when the ship bounces like this.

HAZO

Mama, we've never learned to swim.

FATHER RAT

The sailors are casting lots to find out who is causing the
storm. We'd better hide.

MOTHER RAT

You aren't inferring—

FATHER RAT

If you'd taken my advice, we'd be safe and dry in Joppa.

MOTHER RAT

You always blame things on me. As if the weather was my fault. Can I help it if the forecast was unreliable?

HUZ

Mama, that passenger—

BUZ

The one we saw climbing up the gangplank—

HAZO

He hasn't been praying. He's sound asleep.

MOTHER RAT

Maybe his god is good with storms. Let's go wake him up.

[*They cross to* JONAH]

Nibble his toes, children.

[JONAH *jerks his feet away, buries his head in his arms*]

MOTHER RAT

Wake up, now. This is no time for sleep. We're in the middle of a terrible storm.

FATHER RAT

And liable to perish any minute.

MOTHER RAT

And we need the help of any gods we can get.

FATHER RAT

I don't know who your god is, but those Phoenician gods were always unreliable.

MOTHER RAT

Who are you, and who is your god?

JONAH

I am Jonah, son of Amittai, and I am a prophet. I fear the Lord, the God of heaven, which hath made the sea and the dry land.

MOTHER RAT

Then speak to him. Speak to him at once. My children's lives are in danger in this tempestuous sea.

JONAH

[*Rising*]

Do not I hate them, O Lord, that hate thee? and am not I grieved with those that rise up against thee? I hate them with perfect hatred. I count them mine enemies.

FATHER RAT

That's an odd kind of prayer.

HUZ

Oh, mama!

BUZ

Oh, papa!

HAZO

The ship is going to break up!

JONAH

[*Striding forward*]

Sailors! Take me up, and cast me forth into the sea; so shall the sea be calm unto you: for I know that for my sake this great tempest is upon you.

MOTHER RAT

Oh, no, don't let them do that! He'll drown.

FATHER RAT

If he doesn't, we will.

HUZ

Mama, the sailors are rowing.

BUZ

They're trying to get back to land.

FATHER RAT

They'll never make it. Not in this weather.

HAZO

They're going to throw him overboard!

HUZ

They're picking him up!

BUZ

They have him at the rail.


HAZO

And over!


MOTHER RAT

Don't look, children. Cover your eyes.

[*There is the sound of a tremendous splash, followed by a great splatter of water that sends the rats scurrying off to a final flash of lightning and crash of thunder. Then there is silence and darkness. The darkness is penetrated by a red spotlight, and we see* JONAH *in the belly of the whale. A little fish is swimming around him very curiously*]


LITTLE FISH

What kind of a fish are you?
I've never seen a fish like you before.
You certainly don't look like a proper fish.
You might be a kind of starfish who's lost one arm
But everybody knows they really aren't fish
And are only useful for opening clams.


JONAH

I'm not a fish at all.


LITTLE FISH

Then what are you doing here?


JONAH

I'm not doing anything.

[ 34 ]

I have every intention of not doing anything.
All I want to do is mind my own business.

LITTLE FISH

Well, I'm not interfering with yours, I'm sure.
If there's any interfering you're doing it.
You're taking up a great deal of room.
I am a fish within a fish.
As a matter of fact, I think he probably swallowed
Me by mistake when he was swallowing you.

JONAH

It would have been better if I had drowned.
It would have been more suitable.

LITTLE FISH

That proves you're not a fish.
Fish don't drown.

JONAH

I've already told you I'm not a fish.

LITTLE FISH

What are you, then? Some kind of monster?

JONAH

I'm a prophet.

LITTLE FISH

What's that?

[*The voice of the* WHALE *is heard, surrounding them*]

[ 35 ]

#### WHALE

Silence, little fish. Silence, prophet. I wish to speak.

#### LITTLE FISH

I've met him before. Don't pay any attention to him. He's just a big blow.

#### WHALE

Little fish, we are three days' journey from dry land. At the end of that time I shall vomit forth this prophet, and I only hope my digestion isn't ruined before then. If you aren't careful, I shall vomit *you* forth upon the dry land, too.

#### LITTLE FISH

Oh, no, whale, you need me. You need female companionship in the first place. In the second place you need me to show you where to go. You know how nearsighted you are. You only swallowed me along with the prophet-creature because you couldn't see what you were doing.

#### WHALE

Can *you* see what you are doing, O little, little fish? Can anyone see? Can the stars at night be the eyes of the sky? I do not think that anyone can see very well. But there is no reason not to *hear*. Now listen.

#### LITTLE FISH

[*To* JONAH]

He's always trying to boss people around. But he'd be

absolutely lost without me. Don't pay any attention to him.

WHALE

To whom, then, should he pay attention?
Attend, prophet, without arrogance or condescension.
Nineveh is waiting for your utterance
Whether or not you hold that great city in abhor-
rence.
If you flee to the end of the morning or behind the
corner of night
You will still hear the word of the Lord, for the word
was heard before sight.
Take your fingers out of your ears, O prophet, and
attend.
Your flight is useless. Let your disobedience end.
God has prepared me simply to confound you.
And you are accustomed to God: this should not
astound you.


JONAH

Why don't you digest me or something. It would be nastier
than drowning, but better than having to listen to you.


WHALE

You shall listen to me until you see the light of day.
And that will be when you decide to have not your
way
But God's way.
You will discover that it is not expedient

[ 37 ]

To continue to be so willfully disobedient.

##### JONAH

I never asked to be born. Did anybody consult me about
it? No. But now that I'm here, ready or not, I think I
ought to have a little to say in the matter.

##### LITTLE FISH

You're absolutely right, O Prophet-creature. Don't let
that pompous fish upset you.

##### JONAH

I didn't ask to be a prophet. It wasn't my idea at all. But
I went to King Jeroboam the Second and prophesied as I
was told to do. And ever since then, You've been after me.

##### LITTLE FISH

But he's never seen you before.

##### JONAH

I was not speaking to the great fish.

##### WHALE

Not to me but to him who in his wisdom prepared
Me. I should not have cared
To do this for you, Jonah. I should have despaired.

##### LITTLE FISH

Did he prepare *me* for the prophet, too? I do think that's
nice because I am so extremely beautiful that anyone
around me must feel happier.

Stop talking, O silly little fish,
Or I personally shall see to it that you end up on a
dish.


LITTLE FISH

But did *he* prepare me, too?


WHALE

Yes, it is possible that you, too, are part of God's
preparation.
I myself find it interesting to be part of this strange
oblation.
Realizing that the preparations of God
Are to most of his creatures thoroughly inconceivable,
I have easily learned to believe the unbelievable,
And to accept without question the peculiarity of his
choice.
Though frankly, Jonah, if I were God
I would never have chosen *you* to be a mouthpiece for
my voice.


JONAH

Are you casting aspersions on my ability as a prophet?


LITTLE FISH

[*Pertly, to* WHALE]

Sometimes I think you think you *are* God. You always
seem to know exactly what he's thinking. But you're only
a fish even if you're bigger than I am. Who are you to
think you can speak like God?

#### WHALE

How else should God speak
Except through his own creation?
All creatures great or weak
Live through his contemplation.
He will not lose sight of anyone whom he may seek.

#### JONAH

Big fish, your hide is extremely opaque.

#### WHALE

Hush. I have a frightful bellyache.
I know, O prophet, that God works in mysterious
    ways his wonders to perform,
But I can't see *you* convincing anyone in Nineveh
    he's doing any harm.

#### JONAH
[*Roaring*]

Are you questioning my reputation as a prophet?

#### WHALE

Weren't you fleeing from the Lord, and incidentally
Nineveh, when you were tossed into the sea?
That's hardly prophetlike behavior if you ask me.

#### JONAH

I didn't.

[ 41 ]

### WHALE

And you are, after all, causing the Lord a lot of
trouble

Frightening those poor rats and sailors and annoying
their gods

With storms and winds and then making me swallow
double,

You, and this idiotic little fish who is extremely tickly.

I only hope I don't end up after all this business
being sickly.

Tell me, little fish, if it were *you* he was going after

With prophecies of God's wrath, don't you think your
first reaction would be laughter?


### JONAH

Let me out! I'm going to Nineveh at once! You'll see
whether or not anyone laughs at me.


### WHALE

Be quiet, Jonah. I shall not allow you to interfere
with God's ways.

I'm not as lenient as he is, and you will stay in my
belly the full three days.

On the very borders of that land from which in thy
foolishness thou scurried

As a crab, do I vomit thee forth, though I will not be
hurried.

[*The red light is extinguished and there is a great sound of
gargling waters. Through the darkness,* JONAH'S *voice is heard,
prophesying: he sounds a little like the whale. As the lights*

*come on, we see the birds again; they listen, watch, and applaud*]

#### JONAH

There is no faithfulness in your mouths.
Your inward parts are very wickedness.
Your throat is an open sepulcher.

#### GOOSE

Oh, I'm frightened, I'm scared out of my wits.

#### OWL

Hush, Goose: it is not by beast or bird
That this cry of wrath is sent to be heard.

#### CATBIRD

It's the people of Nineveh should be having fits.

#### JONAH

Art thou better than the populous No
That was situate among the rivers?
Yet was she carried away,
She went into captivity:
Her young children also were dashed in pieces
At the top of the streets.

#### JAY

They are afraid in Nineveh;
They fall on their faces in the street.

Their knees are bruised, their clothes are rent,
They turn from wine, from grain, from meat.


ALL

Repent, O Nineveh, O Nineveh, repent!


GOOSE

But is this what Jonah really meant?
I thought we wanted to see them destroyed!
I thought we were going to be overjoyed!


JONAH

Destroy them, O God;
Let them perish through their own imaginations:
Cast them out in the multitude of their ungodliness;
For they have rebelled against thee.


GOOSE

The lightning has not flashed!
The thunder has not crashed!


JAY

Sackcloth and ashes replace purple and gold.


CATBIRD

The wolf has turned to a lamb in the fold.


OWL

The people of Nineveh have repented.
The great and terrible Wrath has relented.

[JONAH *comes in; he is furious*]

#### JAY

You've done it this time, haven't you, Jonah?

#### JONAH

What are *you* doing here?

#### JAY

We've been waiting for you for three days. When you left
Gath-hepher we thought we'd fly over to Nineveh and see
what was going to happen.

#### GOOSE

Nothing ever happens in Gath-hepher.

#### CATBIRD

Actually, I came for the night life, and I must say it was
all very gay until you arrived.

#### GOOSE

It was *quite* different from Gath-hepher. In Nineveh they
really know how to be wicked.

#### CATBIRD

Style, that's what they have.

#### OWL

Had.

[ 45 ]

JAY

Had is right. I hope you're pleased. You've gone and done it all right.


JONAH

Idiotic bird, what are you wearing? Take it off.


JAY

[*Reaching for her earring*]

Oops, I forgot.


JONAH

I didn't mean that bauble. That—costume. Take it off.


JAY

Oh, you mean the sackcloth and ashes? Can't. Orders of the King of Nineveh. You heard him.


OWL

Let neither man nor beast, herd nor flock, taste anything: let them not feed, nor drink water: But let man and beast be covered with sackcloth, and cry mightily unto God: yea, let them turn every one from his evil way, and from the violence that is in their hands. Who can tell if God will turn and repent and turn away from his fierce anger, that we perish not.


GOOSE

That's what the King of Nineveh said, all right. You sounded just like him.

JONAH

[*Bellowing*]

This is inordinate! I didn't ask you to come to Nineveh
at all, much less join in this excessive repentance.

[*He scowls at the* JAY]

Although yours is more than temperate. That is the small-
est excuse for sackcloth—

JAY

We can take a hint, prophet. If you don't want us around,
we'll leave. Farewell, O Jonah, son of Amittai.

CATBIRD

There's no fun around here any more.

JAY

This sackcloth and ashes is not becoming to me and hides
my true colors. But I'll leave you the earring as a souvenir
of our repentance and your success as a prophet if you
like.

JONAH

[*Striking the earring from her hand*]

Go back to Gath-hepher, faithless fowl. Desert me in my
displeasure. I am exceedingly displeased.

JAY

You are exceedingly difficult to please. Not only did nobody throw things at you, nobody even thought you were
funny.

JONAH

[*Thundering*]

Why should they think me funny?


JAY

There you were with your robe in rags and all those rich important elegant people listened to you. Not only did they listen, they all repented. What more do you want?


CATBIRD

Everybody's fasting and wearing sackcloth and they've closed all the night spots.


OWL

Adieu, Jonah. You are, as a minor prophet, egregiously successful. If and when you return to Gath-hepher, remember that we are your loyal followers even if at this moment we seem to be withdrawing from the formidability of your presence.


JAY

All he means is: we don't know what you're in such a temper about. Well: goodbye, Jonah, son of Amittai.


BIRDS

Yes, Jonah. Goodbye. And congratulations.

[*But* JONAH *has turned away from them, so that he doesn't even see them leave*]

Yes, Lord, I do well to be angry.

I do very well.

I told you so.

Back in Gath-hepher which I should never have left

I told you so.

I would have been willing to come to Nineveh,

And I would have been willing to prophesy their
doom

If I could have depended on your wrath.

But I told you, Lord, back in Gath-hepher

That you are immoderate

And intemperate

And it is not fitting for you to be gracious to gentiles.

They are not your people.

But I will give you one more chance, Lord.

I will sit here on the east of Nineveh and wait

And perhaps you will see fit to bring about the destruction

Of the city.

If it is not suitable for me to associate with Assyrians,

I hardly think it is suitable for you to be so gracious.

[*He sits. The gourd vine appears behind him, brought in by the*
TURTLE]


TURTLE

I have brought the vine out of Egypt, O sullen prophet.
You shall be covered with the goodly shadow of it, for the
boughs thereof are like the goodly cedar tree.

[*He places the vine so that* JONAH *is protected by its shade*]

There. Are you pleased?

JONAH

[*Cautiously*]

Yes. I am pleased.

TURTLE

It is a pleasant gourd, is it not, Jonah? A cooling shadow over your head, a deliverance from your grief.

JONAH

Who is speaking?

TURTLE

[*Pleasantly*]

The voice of the turtle is heard in the land.

JONAH

That, as you should know, refers to the turtledove.

TURTLE

I see no dove talking to you. Poor substitute though I be, earthbound and ludicrous, yet I must ask the courtesy of your attention.

JONAH

I'm not feeling particularly talkative.

TURTLE

Even I know the old saw that a turtle advances only when he sticks out his neck.

Put it back in.

There's no need to be rude. Do you mind if I sit in the shade for a few minutes? It is exceedingly hot.

[JONAH *grudgingly moves a few inches*]

You'd think he was sorry for them.

Sorry for whom?

The people of Nineveh. All that weeping and wailing. All that noisy repenting. The trouble is that he's a gracious God, and merciful, slow to anger and of great kindness. It is unreliable to have so soft a heart.

Do you think that it is easier to forgive than to destroy?

Nineveh is a large and great city. It takes three days' journey to cross from one side to the other. It would not be so simple to destroy Nineveh as you seem to think.

It is easier, prophet, to destroy the entire universe

than to prepare this vine in whose shade we now
relax.

Can you create with all your anger a single leaf?

And yet it was easier to create all the stars in the sky
than to prepare me.

You think he would find it difficult to destroy
Nineveh,

that great city?

A thunderbolt could lay waste to it in three seconds,

but compassion takes eternity.

Pity, Jonah, son of Amittai, is the most violent of all
judgments.

It is easy to destroy one's enemy without suffering,

but to love him is the most terrible of all pain.

And you are afraid of pain.

Sleep well, prophet. I am tired, now.

I have come a long way to you

and I am not accustomed to this much conversation.

[*He withdraws, then puts his head out again*]

All right, worm. The time is now ready for you.

Come, east wind, O hot east wind,

and beat upon the prophet's head

that he may faint.

[*He withdraws.* JONAH *puts his head in his arms in despair.
The* WORM *comes on and eats the vine so that it withers. The*
JAY *enters and looks at* JONAH, *but speaks to the* WORM]

JAY

What did you do that for?


WORM

I was hungry.


JAY

But you destroyed the vine.


WORM

Nothing personal.


JAY

But now the prophet will have no shade.


WORM

I said I had nothing personal against the vine. I have nothing personal against the prophet. I was hungry.

[JONAH *raises his head*]


JAY

This worm here has eaten the vine and destroyed it, O Jonah, son of Amittai. And there's a nasty east wind blowing. It's getting dust in my feathers. It's as bad as ashes.


JONAH

What are you doing *here?*


JAY

[*Shrugging*]

Somehow I didn't want to go back to Gath-hepher without

you. Not when you were in such a bad mood about being so successful in Nineveh. Are you in a bad mood now?

JONAH

[Looking at the withered vine]

A very bad mood.

WORM

If you'll excuse me, I'd better be going.

JAY

Now just you wait, Worm. I'll tell you when you can go and if you can go. I'm hungry, too. Jonah, son of Amittai, do you do well to be angry?

JONAH

I do well to be angry. I do very well. I am angry unto death. It is better for me to die than to live.

WORM

It was nothing personal against you, prophet.

JONAH

[Thundering]

Why did you destroy my gourd vine?

WORM

It's in my nature. I was hungry. There was nothing else to eat around here, and suddenly I saw this delicious gourd . . .

And you destroyed it.

After all, I am a worm and no man.

Why, Lord,
What possessed you
Out among the stars
Out among the wild winds of your universe
Why God
With all of this to occupy you
Or to amuse you if you need amusement
Did you see fit to prepare a worm,
A worm, God,
When you could have been juggling the stars
For my amazement.
For I am amazed.
I did not expect this.
You told me to warn Nineveh
And against my better judgment
I warned them.
Let me die, O Lord,
Ask me not again to frighten people into repentance
And your compassion.
Oh, what you prepared for me, O Lord,
Whales and worms!

Now calm down, Jonah. I'll take care of everything for

you. He ate the vine and you're about to die of heat, so
I'll eat him.

WORM

Have pity.

JAY

[*Chasing him*]
It's in my nature to eat worms.

WORM

Prophet! Spare me!

JONAH

Why should I?

WORM

Eating me won't bring back the vine.

JAY

True. But it will assuage my hunger. Everybody's fasting
in Nineveh and I can't get a bite to eat. I stayed here
because of the prophet and I'm sure he doesn't want me
to go hungry, do you, Jonah?

WORM

O prophet, remember who sent me.

JONAH

That is just what I don't want to do.

But you pitied the gentiles, didn't you?

Certainly not.

You had them throw you overboard lest the ship sink because of your presence and the wrath of your God.

Oh, that! The sailors. It is all right for *me* to have mercy on the gentiles. I am only a weak and foolish prophet, that has been made quite clear. But it is completely unfitting and undependable of God.

And the vine, Jonah, that I ate? You got into a rage at the destruction of the vine, for which you did not labor, nor did you make it grow. So should you not also pity me?

If I pity you, Worm, if I accept my own pity, then I must accept God's pity also.

Is that so difficult?

O Worm, I wanted the destruction of Nineveh.

After having seen that great city? After having seen the
people? After having seen the six score thousand persons
that cannot discern between their right hand and their left
hand, and also much cattle?

JONAH

Let him go, Jay.

JAY

But I'm hungry.

JONAH

Let him go, O foolish fowl.
  I am shaken by pity,
  And it is more terrible than anger.
  What God does or does not do in Nineveh
  Is out of my hands
  As well as my comprehension,
  But I will spare this worm.

WORM

I'm really very much obliged, prophet.

JONAH

I am not obliging.
I think I have sunstroke.

[*He hitches up his robes and prepares to leave*]

JAY

[*Fluttering after him*]

Where are we going, Jonah?

*I* am going back to Gath-hepher. Back to Gath-hepher, Lord, from whence you sent me with all your foolishness of fowl and rats and whales and turtles and worms and also much cattle . . .

[*He turns to* JAY]

Are you still following me?

A prophet, Jonah, needs a friend on a journey.

[*Shrugging*]

Come then. Back to Gath-hepher. Back, O Lord, to whatever preposterousness you may in your incomprehensibility see fit to prepare.

[*They leave*]

**CURTAIN**

# PRODUCTION NOTE

The play, *The Journey with Jonah,* has been performed by the students of St. Hilda's and St. Hugh's School in New York City, and perhaps a few words on how we did it may be helpful. Everything was as simple as possible. We had no scenery, only the dark blue backdrop of the McMillin Theatre, which Columbia University kindly allowed us to use. The costumes, made by one of the sisters of the Community of the Holy Spirit and by the students, were tights and smocks of colors appropriate to each animal, and delightfully imaginative half masks cut out of paper. The rats, for instance, wore brown tights and shirts, and masks featuring long whiskers; the Jay wore blue, the Goose white, etc. A red spotlight thrown on the stage served as the interior of the whale's belly, and two tape recorders were hooked together so that the whale's voice came out with an eerie hollowness. At intervals the whale blew into the mike so that he sounded as if he were spouting. The little fish had long ribbons on each finger and "swam" gracefully around Jonah. All very simple, but quite effective. The vine and gourd was an ingenious concoction with a balloon for a gourd; when the worm "ate" the gourd, a string was pulled which caused a pin to puncture the balloon. The main thing is that there are all kinds of extremely simple effects that the actors themselves think up during rehearsals. Our students did a good bit of thinking about what the play could mean to them, right now, today; we all got into a heated but exciting argument about the turtle's long speech.

My love and gratitude to those who made the first journey with Jonah:

JONAH, *John Bacopulos*

BLUEJAY, *Carla Givens*

CATBIRD, *Diana Leonovich*

GOOSE, *Carla Sayers*

OWL, *Thomas Damrosch*

MOTHER RAT, *Sarah Susan Brodt*

FATHER RAT, *Peter Daniels*

HUZ, *Nancy Ballou*

BUZ, *Carol Peck*

HAZO, *Sharon Sakai*

WHALE, *Grant Beeney*

LITTLE FISH, *Maureen Parker*

TURTLE, *Lorca Morello*

WORM, *Gail Sheffield*

M. L'E.